The Wolf

The prequel to The Keeper Saga

K.R. Thompson

Pre-Publication Copy Editor: J. K. Brooks Publishing.com
Cover Design: Keri Knutson

The Wolf/K.R. Thompson—1st ed.
ISBN-13: 978-1500450694
ISBN-10: 1500450693

DEDICATION

For Erin,
Who is my own Moon, in many ways.

"I shall put her in the sky and there you might always see her ..."

~ THE GREAT SPIRIT

ONE

SWIFT FOOT HADN'T meant to say the words aloud quite yet, but they popped out anyway, "My life began with you." He linked his fingers into the ones that belonged to the girl who walked beside him. He felt the air spark and swirl around them as soon as he touched her hand. The slightest touch brought the magic alive between them.

"No, it didn't begin with me," Shining Star grinned up at him, "You are two winters older than I am, so your life began before I existed."

Swift Foot lowered his head and kissed her. The air snapped and popped around them. Neither of them denied the presence of the magic, though no one else ever noticed the subtle shift in temperature as it warmed, or the sizzle that crackled in the air when the two touched.

Swift Foot didn't agree with her, but he didn't argue either. He felt all he did was exist before he fell in love with Shining Star. To him, that was when his life began.

They walked hand in hand toward the creek. It was their special place to share time alone. Swift Foot stayed silent. When they arrived at their favorite spot, he would ask Shining Star to be his wife. The thought that she might say no had him more anxious than he had ever been.

He played different scenarios through his head of what would happen when she gave her answer. When she said yes, he would be the happiest man in the universe. Yet, he knew if her answer was no, he would be ready to crawl under a rock somewhere and die.

The girl, with whom Swift Foot wished to spend an eternity, interrupted his inward war with himself. "I went gathering yesterday."

Shining Star was the greatest healer his people had ever known. She spent hours every day foraging in the woods as she collected odd bits of herbs and bark from trees. Swift Foot had once caught her up to her knees as she searched the muck of a creek bottom. Her medicine might not always taste wonderful, and more times than not it contained something slimy or smelly, but it always worked. Along with her kindness and gentle touch, she managed to soothe every ailment from caring for the simplest of scrapes to comforting those souls who took their last breath.

Swift Foot looked down at Shining Star to find a small frown mark that creased between her eyebrows. Her serious expression shook him out of his own thoughts, and he started to pay attention to her words. It wasn't often that there wasn't a smile on her face, but now was one of those rare occasions and it worried him.

"I passed Crow Woman on my way back to the village. She had been in the forest gathering, too," the frown traveled down to Shining Star's lips. "That basket was full of poisonous plants. There is only one reason to collect those. She is learning black medicine."

Whatever Swift Foot had been expecting, it certainly wasn't that. He hoped that Shining Star was wrong. He didn't know much about black medicine, other than it was used by those bent on revenge.

Swift Foot had seen Crow Woman watching him with a look of wantonness, more times than he could count. Any time Shining Star was near, the same wishful look always turned to jealousy. Swift Foot sighed. That basketful of plants confirmed Crow Woman was up to no good.

As children, all three of them had been close. Swift Foot and Crow Woman were the same age, born only days apart. In those early years, where one of them would go, the other would always toddle after. Then Crow Woman's younger sister, Shining Star, was born two years later and the three melded into a friendship that lasted until they were teenagers.

As they grew up, other feelings came into play, and Swift Foot and Shining Star fell in love. Swift Foot knew that Crow Woman felt left out as he and Shining Star spent more and more time together. But, as time passed, he realized that her feelings for him had gone beyond friendship and were much deeper than he thought. Crow Woman mentioned it only once, but Swift Foot remembered every word.

"But I love you, too." The emotion in those few words painted them forever in his memory, along with the hurt that showed in her eyes.

"I'm sorry," he had managed to say, "but my own love lies with Shining Star. She is the one with whom I wish to spend my life."

The hurt in Crow Woman's eyes changed to glistening tears. It had taken every bit of his control not to go to her and tell her that it would be all right. In his mind, she was still his friend and he wished her happiness, though he knew that she wouldn't find it with him. He feared her love for him would grow stronger if he offered comfort of any kind, so he stood helpless, and watched the tears run down her face. Then he watched those tears turn into hate.

Crow Woman never spoke to him again after that, and Swift Foot managed to keep a careful distance away from her. He thought that time healed her hurt feelings and that she had moved on, but now he wasn't so sure.

"A storm is coming," Shining Star's words jolted him back into reality. Swift Foot looked up into the darkening sky. Sudden, black clouds rolled above them, blocking out every trace of the sun that had shown only moments before, and a loud crack of lightening muted whatever Shining Star tried to tell him.

Swift Foot tightened his grip on her hand, and they ran down the path toward the creek as the rain came down in torrents. Instead of staying on the path, he dodged to the left and led her away from the creek bank.

They were soaked. The storm pelted down between the trees and hit the ground with enough force that it bounced back up and stung their legs. A few seconds later, Swift Foot found what he had been searching for and jumped into the shelter of a cave, and pulled Shining Star in after him.

Her long, black hair lay in dripping tendrils around her shoulders. As she looked up at him and smiled, the shadows of the cave caused the silver in her eyes to sparkle.

A cold blast of air came from the belly of the cave and she shivered. Swift Foot sat down against the wall near the cave's opening, and opened his arms. In the next moment, the two were cuddled together and sharing their warmth.

As quickly as it came, the storm began to pass, and Shining Star laid her head against his chest. Swift Foot's heart sped up under her touch. He wrapped his arms around her and held her close.

The music of the rain changed as the clouds moved away. The soft, pattering sounds of single drops that fell through the trees took the place of the thunder, and the sun returned.

Light fell on the puddles outside, causing them to glimmer as if they held pools of magic instead of the rainwater that looked so threatening only a short time ago.

Without even having to search for it, Swift Foot had found his perfect moment. He took a deep breath and waited as Shining Star sat up and looked at him. A strand of dark black hair was stuck to her cheek. He brushed it away with his thumb and traced the line of her jaw down to her chin before he took both of her hands in his own.

"You are the only one I love in this life," he whispered. His heart felt like it had moved up into his throat, "I can't imagine my life without you. You are the one who completes who I am. I will love you forever."

Swift Foot watched as a small flicker of understanding began to take shape on Shining Star's face. It was replaced with a sudden spark of excitement that she seemed barely able to contain.

He forgot to be worried about her answer as he gave her a smile and squeezed her fingers, "Will you marry me, Shining Star?"

The object of his affection jerked her hands out of his and fell on top of him as she wrapped her arms around his neck. "Yes, yes, yes," she chanted happily between the kisses that she left on his lips. Then she began planting them on every inch of his face.

So caught up in Shining Star's joy, Swift Foot barely recognized the sounds of movement that came from deep within the cave. The newly engaged couple had managed to stir something up. Muffled, angry sounds and the scraping of rocks against the cave floor were what finally caught Swift Foot's complete attention.

They weren't in the cave alone. Swift Foot didn't know what they had shared the cave with, but he didn't want to find out. His bride-to-be noticed his strange silence, and quickly hopped off him. Together, they stood still for a moment, but heard nothing more.

Maybe it was just an animal we disturbed, Swift Foot thought as they started back toward the village. There had been one bear in particular that his hunting party had searched for and never found. It could very well be that creature, or possibly another, such as a wolf or a mountain lion that were known to inhabit such places.

Just as they reached the path at the creek, a single heartbroken cry echoed across the rocks. Swift Foot wondered—was it an animal in the belly of the cave or someone who hadn't shared in their joy. Only one person came to his mind.

TWO

SWIFT FOOT'S HEART felt ready to burst with happiness. Shining Star was forever his. His new bride smiled at him from across the village. The fringe on her white buckskin dress swayed as she turned to talk to the women who wished them well on their life together.

It felt strange thinking they would now have a life that was their own. They were as two trees that had grown so close that all of the limbs, branches, and roots twisted together as though they were one. Finally, you wouldn't be able to see where one began and the other ended. Now, they would never be apart.

The happy thought showed in his smile as he watched Shining Star bend to inspect a little boy's arm. She pushed her silky, black hair over her shoulder and knelt to the dirt to take a better look. Ever the healer, Swift Foot knew his new bride was intent on inspecting the little boy's scratch. He watched the little mark between her brows deepen in concentration. The boy's injury must have proven to be a small matter, as she gave the little boy a smile, then a playful swat to the top of his head, and sent him on his way.

The sun caught the silver in her eyes, and they sparkled as she looked up at him. He wanted nothing more than to whisk her away from everyone and have her all to himself, though he knew he wouldn't be able to pull it off. The feast was going to start soon, followed by a celebration with dancing.

There was the fact that his new bride had better manners than he did. She wouldn't leave until she thanked every single member of the village. Shining Star had more kindness in her heart than anyone he had known. She was well loved by nearly everyone.

He noticed Crow Woman standing away from the group of well-wishers. The look of contempt that spread across the young woman's face didn't surprise Swift Foot, though seeing the emotion unmasked with such raw hatred caused him concern. Crow Woman was vocal in her opinion of his marriage to Shining Star. She was bold to imply that he should marry her instead. Everyone, including Swift Foot, ignored her jealous ramblings and mumbled threats. Crow Woman was mumbling now as her fingers played with a small amulet that hung around her neck. Crow Woman turned, looked at him with a glare, and then disappeared around the back of the hut.

As he walked toward Shining Star, she gave him a quick gesture toward the woods, indicating she was going to gather some wood as the supply looked as though it was dwindling. He started to go with her, when his brothers waylaid him, smacking his shoulders in congratulations. They were members of his hunting party. Their conversation soon left the topic of his marriage and turned to the bear that had continued to elude their grasp.

"It's a ghost. There's no other way to describe it," one warrior, named Red Hawk, crossed his arms over his chest, "We find tracks, but they only lead in circles, and then disappear."

"No, it is real. No phantom could cause the mess that one has," replied one warrior.

Another chimed in, "It took us two days to clean up after its last feast on our corn."

"Real bears eat food. Ghosts wouldn't leave us a trail, even if it is one that leads us nowhere," Swift Foot agreed, as he tried to shake off the feeling of dread that settled upon him.

He wanted to go to Shining Star, but right now, he was stuck. The hunting party meant the survival of his people, so he needed to stay and listen.

"Perhaps we should lay some traps in the morning?"

Swift Foot nodded absently as the dread deepened and a wave of anxiety overtook him. Whatever they needed, he would be glad to take care of the next day, but now he needed to make sure Shining Star was safe. He took one-step backward in an attempt to escape, and promptly knocked over someone behind him.

"Oh. I'm sorry, Grunt," he apologized as he bent and picked up the toddler sprawled facedown in the dirt. He was instantly forgiven, rewarded with a wide smile that showed a mouthful of dirt, and given the wordless grunt for which the child was named.

"If he ever talks, it will be a miracle," Red Hawk grumbled as he took his offspring out of Swift Foot's arms. "All he ever does is grunt and point, grunt and point. I keep telling his mother she should make him ask when he wants something."

The boy wriggled in his father's grasp, causing Red Hawk to hold him closer.

"You smell of dog manure." Red Hawk wrinkled his nose as he located the dark stain on the boy's leg, which proved it was indeed manure his son had landed in. Without another word, he toted Grunt off with the obvious intent of disposing the smelly child into the care of his mother.

Talk of the bear was forgotten for a time as the subject turned to that of the hunters' families. It was then that Swift Foot managed to escape.

Instinct told him that he needed to find his new bride soon. Something was happening and she needed him. He started through the shadows of the forest, when the scream came that chilled him to the marrow of his bones.

Swift Foot raced through the trees. Adrenaline pumped through his body. He ran so quickly the trees seemed to blur before his eyes. His blood was laced in fear, as he followed a trail marked by torn branches and two sets of footprints. The first set were as familiar to him as though they were his own. The footprints were hers, small delicate marks, made by soft moccasins. But the tracks that crushed Shining Star's prints made his heart drop from his chest, down to his belly. Those prints were familiar, too.

The phantom bear that they had been planning to hunt had become even bolder. Now it was close. And it was chasing Shining Star. Swift Foot spotted a strip of white leather hanging in a pile of thorns, still swaying from the momentum of being torn from her dress.

Anger built inside of him, though it was washed away with a fresh wave of worry as another scream broke through the air. Swift Foot could hear them crashing through the brush ahead and he knew he was getting close.

Please, help me save her. His heart pled in the hopes the Great Spirit was looking down and listening. The direction they were heading would soon lead to the mountain's precipice.

Another crash came from just ahead, along with the breathless grunts of the bear, and Swift Foot knew the next moment would be his chance. The brush and brambles gave way, opening to a choppy, rock facing. Shining Star and the giant black bear came abruptly into view, a few feet below him.

The bear was enormous, taller than any Swift Foot had seen, with massive claws, and long, yellowed fangs. Both bear and woman had stopped for a moment, each staring at the other, waiting to see the direction each planned to take.

Swift Foot glanced around. In his experience, a bear never attacked unless provoked or protecting young. He didn't see any cubs, and he couldn't imagine anything that Shining Star could have done to this animal to cause such rage.

The beast had backed Shining Star nearly to the edge of the mountain and was advancing with slow, deliberate steps. Mighty paws swung in the air at her head. Swift Foot took his chance and jumped from the rock above them. His only weapon, a knife, poised to sink between the bear's shoulders.

In the second that he should have felt the black fur under his body, the image faltered and his hands passed through the illusion of the bear. Instead of finding its intended mark, the knife scored the flesh of a young woman beneath. Tumbling to the ground, Swift Foot landed on a single, jagged stone as Crow Woman fell near Shining Star's feet.

Pain erupted in his side as Swift Foot struggled to stand. He looked up to watch his young bride, with no trace of anger on her face, hold out a hand to help the one who had tried to take her life seconds before. Blood ran from the furrowed cut on Crow Woman's face from her hairline to her ruined eye, and then splashed down her jaw. Enraged by the simple gesture of kindness, she jumped up, shoving Shining Star with all her strength.

Time slowed for Swift Foot as Shining Star fell over the edge of the mountain, and he struggled to reach her. He watched as her arm stretched toward him in an effort to be saved. Her black hair lifted around her face as the wind pushed up from the bottom of the rock face.

His hands brushed the tips of her fingers. He was a second too late. He clung to the edge of the cliff with one hand, still leaning and reaching out with his other as he watched her, his heart dropping in sync with her body as she fell.

Her silver eyes met his right before the end came. She gave him a small, sad smile, as if trying to give him some small comfort before the rocks finished what Crow Woman began.

Her body jarred as it struck the ground below and she lay still. Swift Foot knew her spirit was gone. Then, he heard a scream, and somewhere in his mind, he knew it came from his own lips. Another part of him also registered the dark, evil laugh that echoed across the rocks.

He turned, expecting to see Crow Woman in an ecstatic state of happiness. What he found instead, was a small, black bird hopping around the puddle of blood where Crow Woman had last stood. When he saw the red line that ran down the bird's head, Swift Foot knew that Crow Woman was practicing the blackest of medicines. She was capable of dark magic that he hadn't known existed. His knife lay in the dirt nearby. He grabbed the hilt, throwing it at the bird with an aim to take the life that had taken his love. The pain in his side caused him to miss, and the knife whirled out past the crow into a pile of briars. As the bird flew away, mocking laughter echoed in his ears.

It took Swift Foot a long time to make it down the mountain to his bride. The loose pebbles beneath his feet caused him to stumble and fall every other step. The jagged stones cut into his hands each time he reached out to catch himself. The blood running between his fingers felt warm and sticky. His mind registered the sting of pain from the dirt and the pebbles as they ground themselves deeper into his flesh.

As he neared the bottom of the mountain, he looked at Shining Star's body. No sound came from her. His own gasps for breath and the crunch of pebbles from under his feet were the only things that broke the silence when he fell to her side.

Time stopped as he gathered her into his arms. He leaned her head against his shoulder and stroked her hair. He told her every wish he had held for them in his heart and covered her body with millions of tears. He didn't notice how much time had passed until a cool evening breeze brushed against him and the first shadows of dusk fell upon his face.

It was then that he carried her home.

HIS BROTHERS MET him outside the village. The hunters had just begun to search for the missing couple, thinking that they had gone off together to share time alone. When they saw the broken body of the bride, the questions began, but no answers were given.

Without uttering a word, Swift Foot took Shining Star into his hut, and kept watch over her. He didn't allow anyone to enter and wouldn't eat or drink. Days went by while nights slowly passed, and still, he stayed by her side, refusing to leave her.

The same thought ran through his mind, over and over again. He was in a nightmare—a terrible one. But if he could hold on long enough, if he could keep her there with him, he would wake soon, and Shining Star would be there with him. Alive. Whole.

Then, one night, he saw a figure in the hut. Part of his mind tried to find the logic in the apparition in front of him. He knew his body was weakening. The broken bones in his side were not healing. The lack of nourishment and dehydration were beginning to take their toll. He was ready to dismiss the foggy figure as a figment of his imagination when it seemed to speak.

You can't keep her here. You know that, don't you?

Swift Foot crouched over Shining Star, anger flared in his eyes. Was this thing another dark trick from Crow Woman? He wasn't sure, but he wasn't going to let it take Shining Star from him.

You must live without her now. You have to let her go.

The fog around the intruder pulsed, as if warning Swift Foot not to contradict. Swift Foot held his knife ready but didn't speak. He wanted to believe he was only imagining this unwanted being with its unwelcomed advice.

You asked me to help save her.

Swift Foot nearly dropped his knife. The statement was whispered as if to prove identity and nothing more. The only one Swift Foot had begged for help was the Great Spirit. Surprise was replaced with anger. If the Great Spirit had heard his plea, he should have saved Shining Star. He should never have let her fall.

Swift Foot gathered Shining Star in his arms. He wasn't going to let anyone take her away, especially the one who had held the power to save her in the first place.

You must live … you must …

To Swift Foot's horror, he watched Shining Star's body fade slowly from his arms.

I shall put her in the sky and there you may always see her. You will know she watches down on you and wishes you to live …

The foggy apparition of the Great Spirit faded, much as his own beloved had seconds before, leaving him alone.

He ran out into the night, staring up into the black sky. What he saw there, so very far away, was a perfect full moon. The moonlight danced across the trees, gleaming silver that was a perfect match to the color of Shining Star's eyes. She was watching him.

The broken pieces of his heart were shattered forever.

THREE

HE GAVE HIS people no explanation of what happened. He also chose not to tell them of his plan to barter with the Great Spirit. He didn't think there was any need, for either way the night played out, he knew he would never see them again.

He left that night, disappearing into the forest.

One mountain stood off in the distance. Its peak was the highest. It grazed the heavens. It was the closest point that he could get to his love, now in the inky, deep black sky. It seemed it would be the perfect place to make his presence—and his demands—known.

The trip up the mountain took a great deal of the night, his strength had waned, but anger and determination pushed him up to the giant boulder, far above, jutting out into the night air.

The moon was beyond his reach—so close, yet, so far away. Swift Foot stood on the edge of the rock. A cool breeze greeted him, brushing softly against his cheek. He felt Shining Star had sent the breeze to touch him.

"I am here," he told her softly, looking up into the sky. Then, he took a deep breath, and announced loudly to the Great Spirit, "I have come to speak to you."

The breeze was replaced with a sudden burst of warm air, an acknowledgement of sorts.

He took a step forward, feeling the balls of his feet touch the edge of the rock. He was close now.

"You will put me there with her or I will die!" The raw emotion caused his voice to crack, but he knew the Great Spirit heard his demand.

A lightning bolt cracked from a cloudless sky in front of him, striking the ground below. No whispering voices came to his mind or thundering ones either. It seemed the Great Spirit wasn't in the mood for negotiations. It wasn't the response Swift Foot had wished to hear or see. Still, he stood on the rock, while his love watched him from her place in the heavens.

That was just as well, Swift Foot decided. He would be with her soon, with or without any help. He would never spend a day without her.

Another lightning strike lit up the sky as he lifted his arms out, and fell.

WHEN SWIFT FOOT came to, he was lying with his face in a sticker bush. He realized that his plan hadn't gone as planned. His mind still reeling, he managed to lift his head out of the itchy mess. Then everything changed.

He knew he was still very much alive—still without Shining Star—and trapped within a body that was most assuredly not his own. He realized he was now a wolf. He figured he was *cursed*.

The shock of that realization caused him to sit still. He looked up into the clear morning sky. All traces of Shining Star were gone. A bright sun blinded him in place of the moonbeams that had shone down on him the night before.

Anger roiled through his blood, and he stood. He would try again. The Great Spirit would not stop him. He raced to the top of the mountain with four strong legs that were much quicker than the two he had used to stumble up the mountain the previous night.

He arrived at the ledge, still in a fury. He backed up, readied to take a fast run and leap out into the open air, when he noticed a bug crawling across the path in front of him. Curiosity took over and he sat down on his haunches, watching the tiny creature scurry along.

The pause caused him to consider his options. If he were to jump, he might receive more wrath from the Great Spirit. What if he were to wake up the next time with more legs than he had now? That would definitely not be a happy existence for him, though he wasn't sure that the one he had now was any better. No matter how he felt about it, he was trapped in this life. He decided that he had no choice.

Frustrated, he threw his head back and howled, filling the sky with a song of his heartbreak.

Far below, he saw the wisps of smoke from his village. He sat on the ledge for a very long time and watched. He wanted to go home. That was no longer an option. His people would never recognize him in what he had become. Perhaps if he could explain it to them, he would be able to go back. He cleared his throat and attempted to speak.

The sound from his lips came out as a long whine.

It was useless. He was alone. The loneliness seeped in as the day wore on. Through all the long hours, he hid more of his human self away, and became more of the animal the Great Spirit had bestowed on him.

Hours later, the darkness came, and she came with it. As Shining Star lit up the black sky, he threw back his head and howled at the moon. The air filled with his sorrow and pain. For now, his love was the Moon and he was the Wolf.

FOUR

He stayed by the village for days, out of sight. But with each day that passed, he missed his people more. He knew he would have to leave them before the temptation to make his presence known became more than he could handle. Carefully, he watched them from his hiding place amongst the shadows, leaving not so much as a single track that would tell of his presence. He regretted not telling them of Crow

Woman's magic, though he hadn't found any sign that she had returned. They would never know about her, and there wasn't any way to warn them.

Only he could save them should she ever return. If the past days were any indication, she wasn't coming back. It was possible the wound he inflicted couldn't be healed by her magic. If she were weak, she would be easier to finish. He would have to find her first.

He left his hiding place, intent on finding her. Crow Woman had taken everything from him, and he was prepared to match it—a life for a life. The loneliness in his soul eased as a new purpose took its place and he began searching for her.

Days passed, and then weeks. Nearly every hour in the day was spent looking for any sign or trail of where she might have gone. The few hours he slept, were during the day, for at night he belonged to the Moon, and every second was spent gazing up into the sky.

So much time passed, exactly how much, he never knew. He did not find any trace of Crow

Woman, though he did find spots where he knew she had been. There were dead places in the forest, where no living thing could be found and only dark magic thrived. He kept careful watch on these dark places, but still found nothing that pointed him to where Crow Woman had gone. It was as if she were a dark spirit that could disappear at will, leaving only her magic to remind him of who he had been and what she had done.

It was in these lonely moments that he found kindred spirits in the wolves of the forest. They had accepted him for what he had become. With them, his curse became easier to endure and the pain became easier to forget. He learned what it was to be truly the creature whose body he shared. The wolves showed him the thrill of the hunt, and gave him the sense of belonging for which he ached. He found the more time he spent with them, the less he thought about his people, and the more he thought of Shining Star as the Moon, instead of the woman he loved.

The fear of losing his memories of her forced him to part with the wolves, though he knew he would come back when his buried humanity resurfaced and became too much to withstand. Perhaps, if he were lucky, the Great Spirit would soon grant his place in the sky and he wouldn't have to maintain this careful balance of wolf and man for all of eternity. He decided he would return to the village and bring just a tiny bit of his human nature back to life. He would watch from the shadows and remember.

The sight that greeted him when he looked upon his village gave him pause. While he found the feelings he thought he had lost, there was a sense of dread and fear that washed over him.

As he walked into the village, he could tell the fires had gone out, but the wooden frames of the huts still smoldered from being destroyed. Then, the smell of death overwhelmed his senses. He shook his head, trying to shake the scent away as he slowly made his way through the opening of a barricade. It was the first time he had set foot inside the village walls since he became the Wolf.

The bodies of his people littered the ground. It unsettled him. There were so many of them. Men, women, children—babies. Whoever had attacked them had not been picky in the lives they stole. From the sheer number of the dead, it seemed the only goal of the attack was to kill everyone. He stared at the horror of it all.

He stopped in front of the body of an old man and peered down at him. The wrinkled face looked slightly familiar through the blood, though the features he recognized were known to him long ago on the face of a small child, one who hadn't yet learned to speak. The Wolf realized he had been gone from his village much longer than he knew; *many* years had passed. The old face in which he stared belonged to the little boy who was once known as Grunt.

The Wolf noticed that he was taking shallow breaths. He stilled for a moment, and then took a deep breath, ignoring the stench of death, and concentrated on looking for survivors.

Beneath the strong smoke, his brain registered the faint, unfamiliar scent of strangers. The ones responsible for this destruction had not come from any of the neighboring tribes and they weren't anyone that he'd ever encountered before. He didn't know what they had gained from the destruction of his people, but he intended to find out.

A quick search through what remained of his village revealed there were no survivors. He started tracking the marks left in the dirt. Soft marks left by moccasins led toward the mountains. It gave him reassurance that some of his people might have survived. They must be hidden in the shadows of the forest.

Then there were the deep tracks made by shoes with hard soles heading into a valley, the opposite direction of where his people had fled. These tracks were the ones that he turned to follow.

It was a shame that Crow Woman wasn't so easy to track, he thought to himself, trotting easily along as he followed the marks, packed hard in the earth. Whoever these people were, they had made no attempt to hide their trail. The evening came, casting its shadows, reminding him that soon his Moon would be watching.

He followed the valley as it wound between two mountains, through a meadow, and then into one of the places of dark magic that he had discovered during one of his searches for Crow Woman. The trees seemed to be alive as they worked to stop him, stretching their bare branches out, blocking and snagging at his fur.

He gave a low growl and snapped, and the limbs let him be. The path cleared as the trees moved, and something caught his attention, something out in the clearing.

Whatever vengeance he was seeking had been played out by someone else. The tracks he followed ended in a heap of bloody, lifeless bodies.

It is a day for death.

The Wolf wasn't sure if the thought was his or if it belonged to the massive, black bear that was in the process of snapping its last victim's neck.

The hair rose along the Wolf's hackles as he realized the one in front of him wasn't just any ordinary bear. As if she had just noticed an audience, she turned, facing him.

One endless, black eye stared at him—the other ruined by a familiar, jagged scar.

The one he had searched for, for so many years, stood only feet away. Surprise was in his favor, as Crow Woman didn't recognize him, which was understandable as he was human the last time she had seen him.

After it became obvious that the intruder wasn't leaving, the bear threw back her head and roared in an obvious attempt to scare him away. The Wolf simply glared and stalked toward her, his head bent low in a deep growl.

He was nearly on her when a look of shock flashed across the bear's face. He sprang on her in that moment of recognition, fully expecting to go past the bear's image and touch the flesh of the woman hidden inside as he had so long ago.

Over the years, Crow Woman had grown stronger, and instead of the Wolf sinking his teeth into the woman, his fangs found the bear's neck. He held on. The bear wrapped her paws around him and squeezed. When that didn't work, she flung them both backwards and they rolled, a ball of brown and black fur crashing along the dead leaves and branches.

The momentum hadn't loosened his grip on her neck. If anything, his teeth sank in deeper. The bear roared in fury and sank her own teeth in his flank. The surprise of it startled him just enough that he yipped, causing him to turn loose for only a fraction of a second.

The Wolf bit her again and suddenly found his prey shrinking. His fangs were not the cause of the sudden change in size. Rather, his claws had somehow hooked the leather string of an amulet that hung around her neck.

The amulet fell to the ground, followed by Crow Woman, and then the Wolf. They landed a few feet apart. The Wolf jumped up; ready to attack again, when Crow Woman began to change.

While Crow Woman had landed on the ground looking nearly the same as the last day he saw her, she started to age. Lines appeared in what was once a young face, and then they deepened. Her black hair turned to gray. Without the source of her magic, nature was correcting what time should have taken from her. Her true age showed.

She clasped her hands to the wound on her neck, and hobbled away. The animal in him wanted to chase and finish what she had begun. Yet, after seeing such death, he knew the revenge he had harbored for so long needed to end. Moonbeams painted the dark place in a perfect, silver light, reminding him of the kindness that had been in Shining Star's heart. She would not want him to seek revenge any longer.

Death would come for Crow Woman soon, he decided. Either by old age or her wound, but she wouldn't die by his hand on this night. He would do as Shining Star wished and keep this small part of him human, for now. A gleam in the moonlight caught his eye.

Hidden among the leaves, glowed a bright blue stone. The amulet was waiting for him.

IT HAD TAKEN him time to figure out what he needed to do with the stone. Part of him felt it should be destroyed. Another part of him argued that he should keep it in case Crow Woman came back. If she *did* come back, then it was best if the little blue rock was not there to return her power.

Preoccupied with this new conundrum, he carried the amulet in his mouth and made his way to the creek. He always thought best there, even when he was human. The simple sounds of the water managed to soothe his mind.

He was getting ready to spit the amulet out on the ground and get a drink, when he noticed that he had accidentally stepped on something. A young boy knelt at the water, doing the same exact thing the Wolf had planned to do. Water droplets ran tracks down a sooty, dirty face, and bright, golden eyes looked up at him, startled.

The Wolf gingerly removed his foot from the boy's moccasin.

Sorry, he thought apologetically.

To his surprise, the boy's eyes widened even further, and he didn't run as the Wolf had fully expected him to do.

"That's all right," the boy said, politely.

Now the Wolf's eyes widened. This young boy before him had somehow managed to hear him. No one had done that in such a long time. His mouth opened in shock and the amulet dropped to the ground.

He decided to ask, just to be certain that he wasn't imagining things.

Did you understand me?

The sound he heard, which came from his own mouth, was a whine that varied in cadence.

The boy looked thoughtful for a moment, then picked up the amulet and tied the leather cord together where it had broken, then leaned over and gingerly set it over the Wolf's head.

"I think this was helping you," he said, "Try it again, if you want."

Thank you.

It was nice not to have to figure out how he was going to carry the amulet around anymore.

"You're welcome," the boy grinned at him, teeth showing white in a face of dirt and grime.

What happened to your village?

He knew the boy had come from there by the evidence of the soot and the scent of smoke that clung to him.

The bright smile vanished, "The white men came. For a long time they acted as friends, but they lied." His golden eyes shimmered with tears.

The Wolf stayed silent and waited. He was most impressed with the boy's courage when he raked the back of his hand across his eyes to clear the tears.

The boy continued in a matter-of-fact way, "We tried to stop them, but they still took what they wanted, and then they started killing everyone. There are not many of us left now."

They won't return, the Wolf promised, though he didn't tell the boy why he was so sure. He only hoped the pile of bodies in the dark place had held all of the ones responsible for the massacre in his village. But even if it didn't, he had a plan. And this time—if he were lucky—perhaps the Great Spirit would listen.

The Wolf moved closer to the creek, bent down, and got a drink of water, then settled down next to the boy.

So what do they call you?

A wide smile spread across the boy's face.

"I am Bright Eyes."

FIVE

T HE WOLF SAT with the boy for a
long time in companionable silence,
each lost in his own thoughts. He
didn't know what Bright Eyes was thinking,
though from the occasional frown, he gathered
that Bright Eyes might be pondering the recent
events of his people.

As for the Wolf, he was wondering how to
go about convincing the Great Spirit to let him
help them. He hadn't actually spoken to the

Great Spirit since the night he demanded to be put in the sky. But that had been a long time ago, so maybe the Great Spirit wasn't quite so angry with him now and would listen to his request.

He waited with Bright Eyes until the time came for the boy to head back to the place where his people were hiding. Then, the Wolf made his way back up the mountain top again.

He reached the ledge and waited, thinking perhaps the Great Spirit would acknowledge him in some way. He sat there for a while, watching his Moon.

I miss you.

The thought had gone through his mind at least a million times every night. This night was no different. A cloud passed over the Moon, and then moved over to one side.

The Wolf's presence had not gone unnoticed. A small rumble of thunder came from the single cloud, as if daring the Wolf to make his leap again. The Wolf did not intend to do such a thing now. He sat perfectly still to prove it.

The amulet around his neck glowed a ghostly blue. For reasons he himself did not even know, the Wolf opened his mouth and a voice that he hadn't heard in a very long time—his human voice—spoke.

"I need to help them."

The cloud lightened in color, as if the Great Spirit had decided to listen. The Wolf took a deep breath and continued, "I wish them to have something that would keep them safe."

The amulet shone as bright as a star. The Wolf felt the power that entered it and knew the Great Spirit had given him what he had asked for, and he left the mountain with a happier heart. The Wolf, who had wandered the forest for many years, now had a purpose.

As the sun rose, casting the first rays of light into the sky, he made his way to where his people were hidden.

It didn't come as a surprise when Bright Eyes found him before he reached his people.

"I've come to help. I need to see the elders."

At the sound of his voice, the boy's wide smile appeared. He nodded happily, "Come on. I'll take you there."

As they made their way up the mountain, the boy chattered nonstop.

One would think he regularly speaks to talking wolves, the Wolf thought, amused.

"No, only you," came the answer, as easily as if the Wolf had spoken aloud. "My people will be very happy you came."

The Wolf smelled the scent of smoke from a cook fire the instant before a teenage boy landed in front of them. He was hidden above them in the tree that they had just walked under. A spear was pointed directly at the Wolf's nose, less than an inch away.

"What do you think you're doing?" the older boy demanded, "We only barely escape, and you bring a wolf to us? There will be a pack following him." His angry, golden eyes were the same color of the calm, happy ones belonging to the boy who stood at the Wolf's side.

Brothers, the Wolf noted. "I have no pack," he told the older boy, reassuringly, "and I will not bring your people harm."

"He came to help us," Bright Eyes chimed in as the other boy's eyes widened.

The older one didn't speak. He only nodded and led them onward. The Wolf noticed that the elder brother had managed to stand close enough to his younger sibling that he would be able to protect him should the Wolf change his mind. This one was wary and slow to trust. He would do well in protecting his people, the Wolf thought.

The two brothers and the Wolf made their way to a flattened spot on the mountain. They were greeted by five young hunters holding spears and clubs. A quick word from the older brother let them pass. The people they found beyond were a small group, bedraggled, wounded, and frightened.

"There are no elders now," Bright Eyes told the Wolf solemnly, "All dead. We only have Old Mother." The boy gestured to a wizened old woman with milky white eyes, a short distance away.

The woman lifted her head at the sound of her name, turning her blind eyes directly in the Wolf's direction, "Why have you come to us, Brother Wolf?"

She has a bit of the Sight, the Wolf thought, happy that his people still had this old woman and her wisdom to lead them.

"The white men who came were not men of honor," he said, watching as the old woman nodded her head in agreement, "Those men will never come again; I give you my word." She didn't question his promise but only waited patiently as he continued, "I give you a gift to keep your people safe."

A flat stone lay in the dirt in front of him. He nuzzled it free with his nose, then took his paw and scratched the smooth surface, leaving the marks of his claws. He lowered his head.

The amulet grazed the stone and flashed. "The five hunters and the older brother will be protectors and defenders," the Wolf said, thinking of the brave, young hunters he had just met. "They will be known as the Keepers of the forest and all those within."

The Wolf gathered the stone in his mouth and took it to the old woman. As he dropped it into her open hand, the amulet swung forward, touching her palm. A small shock passed between the two and she placed her other hand on his head to steady herself. After one silent moment, she whispered to the Wolf, "One day, you will be with her. You will be with her when your time is done."

The Wolf stayed still under her touch, waiting for any other sign or foretelling of what his future may hold and exactly how much longer he was going to be stuck in this existence, but any other knowledge that the old woman held, stayed with her. After a small pat on his head, she took her hand away, clasping the stone to her, "Thank you, Brother Wolf."

He inclined his head slightly, a very human gesture. He would be forever grateful to the woman in front of him.

"In the morning, the Keepers of the forest will come," he told her as he turned to run back into the shadows of the forest and wait for sunrise.

THAT MORNING, SIX young warriors awoke. The Wolf watched as his gift awakened in each of them, and their bodies were covered in the mist. When the mist melted away, six strong wolves stood where the young warriors had been. Unlike the Wolf, the young wolves would be able to change back into human form at will.

He knew that the ones he had given his gift would soon have adventures of their own—and each time he would keep his watch over them. His gift would travel through many years, the magic passing from father to son, keeping the legacy alive. There were always six wolves for each generation.

Content in the knowledge that the future of his people was now safe, the Wolf left the six warriors and went deeper into the forest to spend time with the wolves and wait until his time came to join Shining Star.

Being among his people had awakened more of his human self than the Wolf had thought possible. As he watched the Moon that night and howled up into the night sky, his song was not one of sadness, but rather of hope. For one day, he knew he would take his place beside her in the sky.

If you enjoyed meeting the Wolf, Bright Eyes, and the Keepers in *The Wolf* ... you will join them in K.R. Thompson's novel

Hidden Moon

BOOK ONE
THE KEEPER SAGA

THE SECRET OF their people was hidden for hundreds of years. Through each generation, it was a legacy and history carefully kept by six guardians known as the Keepers.

One girl would change their future.

SEVENTEEN YEAR OLD Nikki Harmon doesn't' realize her life is about to change when she moves to a small town in Virginia. As she discovers the Indian reservation that borders her new home, she soon realizes there is magic waiting in the dark shadows of

the forest—the myths and legends she never believed in are real.

When she meets Adam, the leader of the six boys known as Keepers, her dreams become haunted by the mournful howls of wolves and visions of the past and the future.

Befriended by Brian, she becomes torn by her feelings for him and for Adam. Thus begins her journey to learn that she must trust her heart in order to discover a strength inside herself that she never knew existed, while she unearths the deadliest secret of all.

Will she lose her heart to one of them … or will she lose her life?

READ ON FOR AN EXCERPT

ONE

IF ANYONE HAD told me that my life was going to change this drastically, I would have rolled my eyes and told them where they could put that prediction. Everyone's life changes—that's what makes life what it is. But, if I had been told the reason for this life-altering change was that I was part of a legend, and I was an important key to a secret that has lasted hundreds of years, I would have thought that person was insane. Myths, legends, and fairytales were only stories found in books. I didn't believe in them.

And, I was beginning to doubt happy endings existed, too.

I watched tree after tree whip past the window of the passenger seat window. There wasn't anything magical about us driving down the interstate; weaving around the endless range of mountains that stretched out as far as the eye could see.

If I had to describe this move, I would have said that it felt like a death sentence, which was kind of ironic, since death was what brought us here in the first place.

Two months before, my dad died in a car accident. We were left with nothing but a small insurance claim and just enough money to move north to my great-grandmother's house. My great-grandmother, Mae Harmon, whom I'd never met, had died the year before and left us her big, rambling estate.

"We're gonna be okay," the words that came out of my mom were not convincing, "This is going to be good for us."

Neither one of us believed that, I thought, listening as her tone fell flat.

"Yeah, we'll be fine." I tried to sound optimistic as I kept my face to the glass so she couldn't see the tears that filled my eyes.

The road curled, and then plunged us into darkness as we started through a tunnel carved into the side of a mountain.

"When you head through Big Walker Tunnel, Nikki Harmon, you've almost made it into the heart of the mountains. That's when you'll find the forest." I couldn't remember how many times my dad had told me that, as if he were giving me directions should I ever need to find my way.

It wasn't so much he was giving me specific directions to the town or even to the house. Rather, it was how I would find my way to the thousands of acres of national forest that ran for miles, surrounding everything. The town, the house, even the interstate were tucked away in that forest. I never understood what he was telling me to find. My one regret was that I hadn't asked him what he'd meant. Now, it was too late. He was gone and I'd never know.

The exit was coming up with a small green sign pointing the way—Bland.

You can say that again, I frowned. It *was* bland. There wasn't even a 'welcome to' in the greeting, or a listing of the population. That sign seemed to say it didn't want us here as much as I wished we didn't have to be.

As the car slowed down for a stop sign, my little sister woke up from her nap in the back seat.

"Are we there yet?" Emily brushed her dark brown curls from her eyes. Fred, her raggedy teddy bear and constant companion, was clutched in her other hand.

"Almost," Mom answered, "Just a few more minutes."

The road curved, taking us away from town and civilization. The mountains became taller and the trees came to the pavement.

After another mile or two of nothing but forest, a small building popped into sight.

As we turned down the gravel road beside it, I saw a carved wooden sign with an emblem of a howling wolf. "The Village," I read aloud, "I wonder what that is?"

"The Indian reservation runs behind it, so the building has to belong to them. Maybe it's an old sort of trading post of some kind. I'd say that the school takes field trips there."

My mother's words sunk into Emily's brain. "Indians," she squealed, "I like it here. I wonder if they'll teach us to shoot arrows."

I grinned. Six year olds were not hard to please. Placate the kid with Indians and she will love the place, sight unseen. I caught the smile tugging at the edge of my mother's lips. It was the first time since we'd left that I'd seen her smile.

The ruts in the road made for a slow, bumpy ride and gave us plenty of time to look at a small two-story house near the road.

"That's a cute house," I said as I took a closer look, and Mom navigated us around a huge pothole. The house was small but seemed well kept. The windows had little boxes where bright, cheery flowers bloomed in bursts of pink and yellow. The swing on the porch swayed in the breeze. Whoever lived there had taken pride in their home.

"Your grandmother gave a half acre to a woman a few years back. She told your father that she was a nice woman who was just down on her luck and needed a place to call her own. I think she called her Anita, but I can't remember a last name. It's been too long. Anyway, the house must be her place. Maybe we can go introduce ourselves once we get settled in."

As we drove further down the lane, I could make out the outline of a house in the trees. Then, it came into full view.

Our house didn't look as loved as that little house a mile back, I thought. Paint was peeling from every visible inch and the sagging roof over the porch gave the house a sense of foreboding. One downstairs window had duct tape across it, making it look like the house had lost an eye.

Awesome. We've inherited a horror house, I thought as I got out of the car to look around. The house had been in the care of a real estate agency since my grandmother's death. I had overheard my mother talking to them, being reassured everything was in good condition and ready for us to move in. Apparently, whomever she was speaking to, liked to live in spooky, broken houses.

I made a circle around the house and came back to the car. My mom still hadn't gotten out. She was gripping the steering wheel so hard her knuckles had turned white.

"Mom. Hey," I tried to get her attention as I opened the driver door and tried to tug her out of it. She felt as if she were concreted into the seat. I was beginning to think I would need a crowbar to pry her out. After a couple seconds of hard tugging, I managed to get her to stand. I decided now was the time to point out every possible good thing I could find.

"Look how huge this house is. Emily will have tons of room to run around. We'll get it fixed up, and then think of all the cookouts we can have in the yard. And hey, if it's raining, then we'll just eat on the porch. We'll get us some rocking chairs, maybe even a hammock. And we could sit here and drink lemonade in the summer," I was wracking my brain trying to think of things that people would do in the middle of nowhere. I should have googled this place before we came. We weren't anywhere close to civilization. I felt like a real estate agent trying to sell something that no one in his or her right mind would want.

I could have strangled that real estate agent; I frowned.

"Do you think it's going to be okay, Nikki?" My mom said as she turned to me. She had a look on her face that was half-hopeful and half-skeptical, as if she wasn't sure she should believe me.

I stretched my fake grin back across my face as far as it would go. I figured I was showing her every tooth I had. Once in grade school, I had smiled like that and a boy told me that I looked like the jack-o-lantern that his dad carved him every year at Halloween. I didn't figure it to be my most convincing smile, but it was all I had now. It must have worked a little because she calmed, and began looking at the front of the house.

"Can we go in, Momma? Can we please? Can we go pick out our bedrooms now?" Emily begged as she hopped from one foot to the other. Her little brown curls bounced around her big brown eyes like tiny brown corkscrews.

Mom bit her bottom lip for a second, and then she smiled, "I guess we may as well see how bad it is. Then, I'm going to call that real estate woman. I know we had a clause in that agreement that everything would be kept up, and this definitely isn't kept. When I'm through, she'll know my name is Brenda Harmon. Let's go inside."

The first thing that caught my attention when we stepped inside was the big staircase that spiraled to the upstairs. Emily ran up the steps and started claiming her room as soon as she hit the top step. I followed her up as Mom finished looking through the downstairs rooms. I found Emily in the room she had claimed and walked down the hall into a bedroom that looked out to the woods on the side of the house. In an effort to be as happy as my sister, I played along and announced my choice.

"This one's mine." I said at the top of my voice.

Emily ran across the hall to see the room I had picked. She crinkled up her little nose in disgust.

"That's the little one," she said slowly, as if she needed to explain it to me, since it was obvious that I didn't understand. "The one down that way is a lot bigger. Don't you want that one?" She pointed a finger down the long hallway toward the other end of the house.

"No, I like this one," I told her. "It's plenty big enough. It's twice as big as my old room."

"Yeah, I guess so."

She wandered over to my window, went up on her tiptoes, and pressed her face to the dirty glass to peer out.

"I know why you like this room. You can look for Indians easier over here, right?"

"Yeah, kid, that's right. And, I'm not trading, so get on out of here. Go find something to explore," I swatted her butt as she giggled and ran past me.

Yep, I can watch for Indians, I smirked. I had my own private door to the upstairs bathroom. I walked in, turned the knob on the sink, and expected nothing. The water that came out in a steady flow surprised me. It was cool and clear, so I splashed my face and looked into the mirror above the sink.

Water droplets clung to my eyelashes as I inspected the reflection staring back at me. A wild, blonde mass of chaos rioted around my head, but my brown eyes were clear and stared back at me with the complete calm I felt in spite of my new circumstances. At sixteen years old, I had already learned a lot about life changing suddenly.

I decided to try the rest of the faucets in the bathroom. The hot water chugged out brownish goo before it ran clear. All of the faucets and the toilet were in working order from what I could tell. I ran down the stairs and looked up to make sure the water I had just sent down the pipes wasn't going to leak on my head.

So far, so good, I thought.

My mom finished a conversation on the pink phone attached to the wall. She hung up and turned to me, "That was the real estate agent; she claimed that they didn't know the house was in that bad of shape. They're going to fire the man who was in charge of it. She's going to send someone out in the next day or so to take a look." She nodded toward the pink phone, "The landline is all that's working, and I don't have a signal on my cell."

I pulled my own phone out of my pocket. Nothing. Not a single bar of service.

"Well, that's lovely," I muttered, then looked back up at Mom, "I'm going to see if I get anything on it outside."

I walked in circles in the yard. I held my phone over my head and I twirled it around my knees, but I couldn't find the slightest hint that my cell phone was ever going to work again.

You'd think this place would have a cell phone tower, I thought irritably, as I headed toward the backyard to try my luck there.

As I walked along the edge of our yard that bordered the forest, the fine hairs on the back of my neck started to stand on end. It felt like something was watching me.

THE FOREST CALLED to him. He felt the whisper of the wind against his skin, the caress of the tall grass that brushed his legs. The forest was green before, but now it seemed vibrant. He reveled in his body. His sight was so much clearer when the animal took over. He could see every leaf in detail, every bit of moss that grew on each tree as he ran.

Am I running? He wondered. It didn't feel like it, as it didn't take much effort at all.

It seemed the forest wanted him. It belonged to him, welcoming him like a long lost friend.

He knew she was here, too. Yet, the hiker didn't belong, not as he did.

He heard her. Her running steps seemed to echo through the trees, but he wasn't worried. She couldn't escape him. He was faster, and he was in no hurry. He would savor every second. Adrenaline coursed through his body, making him want to give chase. He smiled. No, he would do this slowly; it would be exceptional. She was special, after all. She was his, only his. No one would take her away from him.

He could taste her fear in the air and it excited him, coursing through his veins like a drug. He longed to take her essence, to make her part of him, forever. He wished this feeling would last an eternity.

She had stopped. She wasn't running anymore. He didn't see her, but it didn't matter. The animal in him sensed her. There wouldn't be any hiding, at least not on her part.

Finding her would be child's play, he thought, as he crept through the trees as silent as a ghost. Every instinct told him she was close, and his muscles grew taut in anticipation.

With effort, he made himself slow down, to come to a stop. His cold dark eyes scanned for his prey. He could hear her, her labored breaths, coming fast and hard. He was close now. So close.

A slight movement to the right caught his eye. He spotted her then, cowering behind a tree like the pitiful, helpless prey she was. He noticed she hadn't seen him; he stood still, watching her with eyes that weren't human.

She was shaking, small tremors ran the length of her body, her eyes darting back and forth, searching until she saw him. He stepped toward her, forming an evil smile that became a snarl. Her eyes widened in terror as she watched the fur grow over his arms and legs, as his eyes slanted into those of an animal, and the last traces of humanity vanished. She backed up, never taking her eyes off his.

"Please. Please don't," she tripped over a vine, falling down hard on the forest floor. Her eyes squeezed shut. This final, pitiful act drew him toward her. The temptation was just too great now. He could resist it no longer. He could no longer play the game. It had to be now. This was their moment. It belonged to him and this woman in front of him. He knew in that instant, she was his, and would stay his, forever.

Her final cry echoed through the trees.

Disposing of the body wasn't quite as much fun, he decided. They always seemed to run the opposite direction of where he wanted them to go. He always had to backtrack anytime he made a kill.

He sighed, heaving what was left of her on his shoulder as he walked through the forest. He had to be careful as the tree branches were swatting at him now. Nature never did like it when he hunted the hikers. He knew in a day or two, it would forgive him and welcome him again as if nothing happened. That was one of the perks of being a creature of nature. It always forgave him.

His journey led him along the edge of the forest. Usually, he didn't mind this part of his walk since it brought him close enough to see the two houses that sat near the dirt road. He didn't notice anything unusual as he passed the first one, but when the second one came into view, his blood ran cold.

The house that should have been vacant held a small car in its driveway. He dodged farther into the underbrush and felt the briars dig into his clothes. He cursed under his breath as a single thorn scored the flesh of his upper arm. The small, sharp pain quickly scabbed and healed before the thorn was pulled from his body.

He shifted his burden around on his shoulder as he ducked down behind a bush. There, in the back yard, he saw the girl. Then the fury came. His body covered in mist as the animal awoke, ready to hunt. She was close enough to the woods that he could get her without anyone knowing. She was staring into the woods, as if she knew he was there.

He was almost ready to grab her, when a woman came out on the porch.

"NIKKI, GRAB SOME of the cleaning stuff out of the car when you come back in."

"Okay," I answered, running back to the front yard in record time since the back yard had just freaked me out.

There isn't anything there but trees. You're just being silly; I chided myself as I grabbed one of the boxes out of the trunk. You have an overactive imagination.

Once I was back inside the house, the weird feelings left, and I trudged the box upstairs to my mother, who stood in my room.

"The moving guys are supposed to be here tomorrow, so we'll worry about cleaning more when we get up in the morning. Besides, it's going to be dark soon. We'll all stay in your room tonight since it's the smallest," Mom said as she grabbed some cleaner, "I'll take the bathroom. You take this one."

When she left, I started cleaning some of the grime off the window. Then, I saw him.

A boy that seemed to be my own age, stood just inside the edge of the woods, staring up at the window. He wore a pair of jeans that fit snugly over his long legs, and a black tank top showed off the lean muscles in his arms. Those arms also happened to be folded across his chest, as if he didn't like what he saw. His long, straight hair hung to his waist, and was so black that it gave off a blue hue in the places where the sunlight touched it.

No emotion showed on the boy's face. He just stared at me. Thinking he might be waiting for me to make the first move, I moved my hand to the glass, and gave a wave.

He didn't move.

"Nikki, I need some more floor cleaner. That bathroom's a mess. What are you doing?" Mom stopped, as she came around the corner through the door.

"There's a boy outside. Right there at the edge of the woods. He's looking up at me," I said, moving away from the window so she could look.

"Oh? Where? I don't see anyone," she peered through the dirty glass.

"He's gone. He was right there a second ago," I squinted at the trees. There was nothing there. Nothing showed where someone stood seconds earlier.

"He was probably just curious, honey. After all, we are the new neighbors now. They just like to keep an eye on who is moving in around them. Now, how about helping me find some more stuff to clean with, eh? I'm starting to think that sleeping bag is going to feel comfortable tonight."

That night, I dreamt of the Indian boy.

I could see him sitting with others in a circle around a fire. They were all talking. I couldn't hear what they said, but it didn't seem to matter. I was floating around the fire, trying to get closer to the one I had seen outside my window. He was the one I wanted to see. He was laughing and talking to the boy beside him. He didn't look as intimidating as he had out the window. He seemed at ease here. I floated closer to get a better look. I saw the muscles in his shoulders tense as he turned and stared straight into me. He looked shocked for a split second—the same guarded stare that I had seen on his face earlier, returned. I should have backed away, but I was frozen as I stared into the most unusual eyes I had ever seen.

They were the color of liquid amber, with small black flecks spotted here and there. It was as if someone had melted gold, and flicked small shiny bits of onyx around in them. They were beautiful. It was too bad this was a dream, I told myself. He wasn't close enough for me to see his eyes earlier, but no one had eyes like that. I knew I was dreaming. I looked at him again. He was angry. The muscles in his jaw tightened, making his high cheekbones even more pronounced. His eyes narrowed in suspicion as he stared back at me. I backed away, floating back away from the circle, away from the fire, and into the darkness.

I awoke to the sound of a wolf's mournful howl in the distance. Cold chills ran down my spine as I burrowed down deeper in my sleeping bag, and stared up into the faint moonlight that fell through the window.

Look for more books by K.R. Thompson

Hidden Moon

BOOK ONE
THE KEEPER SAGA

Once Upon a Haunted Moon

BOOK TWO
THE KEEPER SAGA

Connect with K.R. Thompson
at her website—

http://authorkrthompson.wix.com/thekeepersaga

And Facebook—

http://www.facebook.com/thekeepersaga

ACKNOWLEDGEMENTS

TO MY READERS—without you, this series would not exist. You are the ones who keep me inspired and writing. You've known my characters nearly as long as I have, and love them every bit as much. To each one of you, thank you for spending time in my world. I shall do my best to keep you entertained during your stay.

TO MY HUSBAND AND SON—thank you for your understanding, love, and support. Your faith in me always carries me through, and that means more to me than you will ever know. I love you both, forever.

TO MY PRE-PUBLICATION SERVICE— J. K. Brooks Publishing. Thank you for the patience and attention to detail that brought my words to life and made this story beautiful. In particular, to Pam B. Newberry, words cannot convey my gratitude for all your wisdom you showed me. You took time to teach me with care, so that I will grow as a writer. I am proud to call you teacher and friend.

TO MY GRAPHIC DESIGNER— Keri Knutson, each time that I think that you cannot surprise me any further, you manage to astound me. You've taken every strange request that I've thrown at you, and created something beautiful. You, my dear, are awesome.

TO MY BETA READERS—Melanie Lee, Tearsa Edwards, and Kim Fields, your feedback and suggestions for this story have been invaluable. I am honored to have you as my readers. Thank you for believing in my world.

TO MY AUTHOR FRIENDS and the members of the Writing Writer's group—from you, I've learned many things. The most important is the value of friendship. Thank you for your support and advice. May magic always find your words and bring your stories to life.

ABOUT THE AUTHOR

K.R. Thompson was born and raised in the Appalachian Mountains. She resides in Southwest Virginia with her husband, son, three cats, and an undeterminable amount of chickens.

An avid reader and a firm believer in the magic of nature, she still watches for evidence of Bigfoot in the mud of Wolf Creek.

Made in the USA
Middletown, DE
04 February 2016